This ELMER book belongs to:

· · · · · · · · · · · · · · · · · · · ·

For Flynn - my first grandson

This paperback edition first published in 2013 by Andersen Press Ltd.
First published in Great Britain in 2006 by Andersen Press Ltd.,
20 Vauxhall Bridge Road, London SW1V 2SA.
Published in Australia by Random House Australia Pty.,
Level 3, 100 Pacific Highway, North Sydney, NSW 2060.
Copyright © David McKee, 2006
The rights of David McKee to be identified as the author and illustrator
of this work have been asserted by him in accordance with
the Copyright, Designs and Patents Act, 1988.
All rights reserved.
Colour separated in Switzerland by Photolitho AG, Zürich.
Printed and bound in Singapore by Tien Wah Press.

10 9 8 7 6 5 4 3 2 1

British Library Cataloguing in Publication Data available.

ISBN 978 184270 751 7

This book has been printed on acid-free paper

ELMER
and AUNT ZELDA

David McKee

Andersen Press

Elmer, the patchwork elephant, had just started playing hide-and-seek with his friends when his cousin, Wilbur, appeared.

"Elmer!" cried Wilbur. "Have you forgotten? We promised to visit Aunt Zelda!"

"Oh yes," said Elmer. "I had forgotten. Come on, we'd better hurry."

"Aunt Zelda has moved, hasn't she?" Elmer asked
Wilbur. "I wonder why?"
"I don't know, but she's getting old," said Wilbur.
"And deaf," said Elmer.

After a while they came across a group of older
elephants, laughing happily.
"I bet Aunt Zelda is among them," said Elmer.
"Play one of your voice tricks, Wilbur. Shout
'Hello' from behind them."

Wilbur could play magic tricks with his voice.
He could make it come from places where he wasn't.
"Hello, everyone!" he called. His voice came from behind
the elephants. They all turned towards the sound.
All, that is, but one: Aunt Zelda.
"Hello, you two," she called.
"Hello, Aunt Zelda," said Elmer. "I knew you'd be there."
"Saw a bear, dear?" said Aunt Zelda. "How interesting."

The other elephants crowded round, eager to meet Aunt Zelda's nephews and to have more voice tricks. But Aunt Zelda called out, "Come on, I want to show you two round."

"Sorry, Aunt Zelda," said Elmer. "We didn't know you were waiting for us."

"Fuss, dear?" said Aunt Zelda. "Who's making a fuss?"

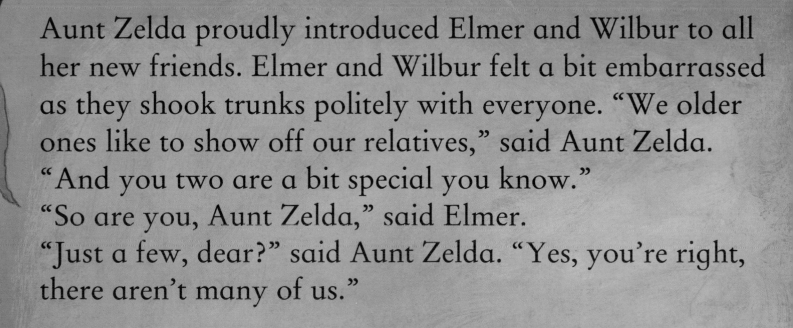

Aunt Zelda proudly introduced Elmer and Wilbur to all her new friends. Elmer and Wilbur felt a bit embarrassed as they shook trunks politely with everyone. "We older ones like to show off our relatives," said Aunt Zelda. "And you two are a bit special you know."

"So are you, Aunt Zelda," said Elmer.

"Just a few, dear?" said Aunt Zelda. "Yes, you're right, there aren't many of us."

Aunt Zelda stopped at the bottom of a hill. "That's where I used to live," she said. "Up there where Tiger is going."

"Hello, Tiger," she called. "I've moved. It was too steep for me up there."

"Good luck in your new place," called Tiger.

"Blue face?" said Aunt Zelda. "What is he talking about?"

Their walk took them by the waterfall. "So you moved because your old place was too steep?" asked Elmer. "And a bit lonely," said Aunt Zelda. "I've lots of friends where I live now. We have lovely walks together, just like we are now. Only here, with that noisy waterfall, you can't hear yourself speak!"

"Time for a rest," said Aunt Zelda. "This is one of our
favourite spots. We sit and talk about memories of when
we were young. You'll do the same one day."
"I'll bet your stories make them laugh," said Elmer.
"Bath, dear?" said Aunt Zelda. "Of course we do,
but not here!"

A bit further on they stopped to look at their reflections in the water. "Look at us," said Wilbur. "Each different from the other."

"But more like each other than like other elephants," said Elmer.

"That's what's known as 'family'," said Aunt Zelda.

When they got back to Aunt Zelda's friends, Wilbur
did some more voice tricks to amuse everyone.
Then he and Elmer set off on their separate ways home.
As they were leaving, Elmer called, "Goodbye, Aunt Zelda,
we'll come again."
"Rain, dear?" called Aunt Zelda. "Yes, maybe later on."

"There you are, Elmer!" said his friends when he got home. "You've won. We searched everywhere for you. Where did you hide?"

"Hide?" said Elmer. Then he remembered they had been playing hide-and-seek. "A secret place," he said. "I might use it again one day."

Read more ELMER stories

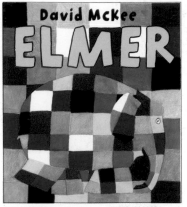

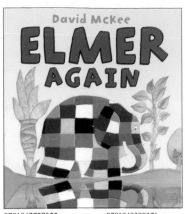

9781842707319 (paperback)   9781849399296 (eBook)
Also available as a book and CD

9781842707500 (paperback)   9781849399371 (eBook)
Also available as a book and CD

9781842707838 (paperback)   9781849399418 (eBook)
Also available as a book and CD

9781842709504 (paperback)   9781849399388 (eBook)
Also available as a book and CD

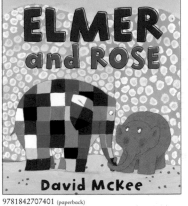

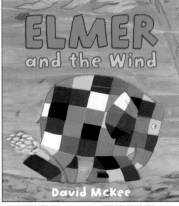

9781842707401 (paperback)

9781842708385 (paperback)   9781849399401 (eBook)

9781842707739 (paperback)   9781849399432 (eBook)

9781842707494 (paperback)

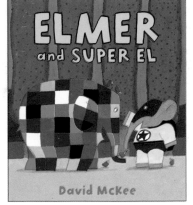

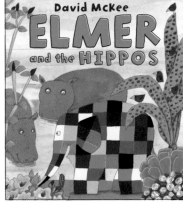

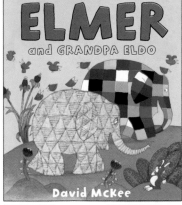

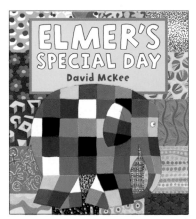

9781849394574 (paperback)   9781849399289 (eBook)

9781842709818 (paperback)   9781849399500 (eBook)

9781842708392 (paperback)   9781849399449 (eBook)

9781842709856 (paperback)

Elmer titles are also available as Apps.

Find out more about David McKee and Elmer, visit:

www.andersenpress.co.uk